Pickles, Please!

A dilly of a book by Andy Myer

Books published by Running Press are available at special dis-
counts for bulk purchases in the United States by corporations,
institutions, and other organizations. For more information,
please contact the Special Markets Department at the Perseus
Books Group, 2300 Chestnut Street, Suite 200, Philadelphia,
PA 19103, or call (800) 810-4145, ext. 5000, or e-mail
special.markets@perseusbooks.com.

ISBN 978-0-7624-4018-4
Library of Congress Control Number: 2010935090

E-book ISBN: 978-0-7624-4245-4

9   8   7   6   5   4   3   2   1
Digit on right indicates the numbers of this printing

Typography: Typography of Coop

Published by Running Press Kids
an imprint of Running Press Book Publishers
A Member of the Perseus Books Group
2300 Chestnut Street
Philadelphia, PA 19103-4371

Visit us on the web!
www.runningpress.com

Pickles, Please!

A dilly of a book by Andy Myer

RP|KIDS
PHILADELPHIA · LONDON

Alec Smart loved pickles.

Big pickles, small pickles, round pickles, sliced pickles.
He loved sweet ones, sour ones, salty ones, and spicy ones.
He liked them made from cucumbers, tomatoes,
beets, and onions. Even watermelon!

"It isn't good to eat so many pickles," said Alec's Mom.
"You'll grow up to be a small green man
who smells like vinegar."

"I'll smell PICKLICIOUS,"
replied Alec.

"Stop eating so many pickles," remarked Alec's Dad. "You'll turn into a pickle some day."

"They'll call me PICKLICIOUS," laughed Alec.

And not one of Alec's friends at school understood
his fondness for pickles.

"I don't care. I still think they're PICKLICIOUS!!"
replied Alec.

But he DID care.

"Why doesn't anyone else like pickles as much as I do," sighed Alec.

One day Alec saw a truck filled with cucumbers waiting for a light to turn green.

"THAT's the place for me!" thought Alec.

He climbed on the truck.

KIDS... Never climb on a cucumber truck without calling home first!!

The driver honked.   The gates opened.

They rode into the factory.

Everything smelled of vinegar and garlic.

MMMMMMM! Picklicious!!

Distilled Vinegar

NICHOLS PICKLES

Alec and the cucumbers had a shower.

They were sorted by size.

And they were about to drop into a very large pot of dill pickles.

Alec felt someone grab his shirt. He swung HIGH in the air.

"Well, hello," said a woman. "I'm Inspector 105.
You don't look like a very
promising pickle."

"I'm Alec Smart," said Alec.

"And why were you in a load
of cucumbers?"
asked Inspector 105.

"I think pickles are PICKLICIOUS!"
explained Alec, "though no one else
understands why."

After some thought, she replied,
"Hmmm. Come with me."

Alec and Inspector 105 walked through the factory.
They finally came to a stop at a green door.
"This is the president of Nichols Pickles," she said.

She knocked.

"Come in," grumbled a voice.

"Mr. Nichols, this is Alec Smart,
someone you should meet,"
said Inspector 105.

"Why are you here, Alec Smart?" asked Mr. Nichols.

"I love pickles so much, but it can be lonely," explained Alec.

"And why do you love them so much?"

BOOM CRUNCH

I love that if you put your hands over your ears when you chew pickles, it sounds like THUNDER!

But mostly, I love them because they are

PICKLICIOUS!!

Then all at once, he yelled,
"That's the word I've been looking for!"

"Tomorrow we have a float in the first Annual Pickle Day Parade, and we still don't have the right slogan for our banner. Thank you, Mr. Alec Smart!"

The next day Alec marched at the front of the parade with the Nichols Pickles Company. His parents were very proud. His friends were very surprised.

And the next day, Alec's end of the lunch table was very crowded with friends who smelled of vinegar and garlic.

They're PICKLICIOUS!!